That Tantalus

That Tantalus

William Bronk

I am William Bronk, have been raised to believe
the personal pronoun plus the verb to be
and a proper name said honestly is fact
from which the plainest narrative begins.
But it isn't fact: it comes to this. Is it wrong?
Not wrong. Just that it isn't true.
No more than the opposite is true. That "I" —
as arbitrary as the proper name; a role
assumed from the verb to be as though to be
were all assumption, were willed, and of course it is.
And anyone fooled is fooled. Do as you will.
It doesn't matter. What happens to us is not
what happens. It isn't by us. We feel it there.
Listen. Something is living. It is not we.
Aren't we that Adam, still, from whom we are?
The garden is here. I have no way to eat,
have never eaten. I round that fruit,
I push against the branches of that tree.

The Elizabeth Press
New Rochelle, N. Y.

Acknowledgements:

The poems collected here first appeared in
these publications: ELIZABETH, FOR NOW,
NEW DIRECTIONS, ORIGIN, THE PARK, &
PROMETHEAN.

This book is produced with the aid of funds
granted the publisher by the
National Endowment for the Arts.

Printed at the Press of Villiers Publications Ltd
Ingestre Road. London, NW5, England

Contents

THE FREEDOM WE FEEL

Like several hours added to the night, or days
put on to the year: the strangeness. Like that.
Not longness, length is nothing. Rather, the lack
of sequence. Broken cycle. Events occur
aside from time. One thing rarely leads
to something else, or follows it. One finds
that sequences are formed, or can be said
to form, but hardly matter. Random things,
the non-sequential, disperse and overwhelm.
Order casts us loose. The strange world.
Nothing we understand. One might control,
influence a little at least, a lesser world,
delimited from this and formalized.
Here, there is no control. The freedom we feel!
Look! See that man? He thought of life
as something happening to him, but he sees it go on
as it must have always gone on — near but away.
If life may be said to happen, it is not to us.
There is a scheme for things to happen in
which we arrange, suggesting this were life
and holding off, or meaning to hold off,
the awful happening outside the scheme
which happens, but not to us, if it happens at all.
We watch a little; nothing can happen to us.

ON THE STREET

The west side of the street is fallen away.
We can look at the river through the sudden openings.
Ruin bares us. The burrows of animals
are drawn like this in diagrams — sometimes
perhaps, in fact. We face the river-bank
and look at the river, pleased, but feeling the half
hollow in which we stand, where fire and rot
have opened as though a fault, made section of the town.
Or the street was a fosse: that fortification gone,
we feel our nakedness, but stay secure
as before. Nothing notices us of what
we must, one time, have thought would notice us
but the street would save us from, would hide us in,
and occupy us so long as we occupied it.
We are neither — man is neither — here nor there
but we want to be, we make up ways to be:
this street, the buildings on it, side and side,
inside, outside, east and west, see here!

Or death, we make a lot of death. We can say
we were living, make death definite enough:
what went before was life, we had it, and one
to come — celestial cities, streets of gold.

Well, otherwise we tend to vague
at the edges. And the center — do you know where the center is?

UNCLE WILL

Towards the end, when his sullen stomach begrudged
all provender almost whatever, he kept
on planting gardens, still, for years. He said,
"I like to see it grow. You eat the stuff;
I can't, but I like to see it grow."
He'd tell me to put the phosphate to it, and gave
an extra syllable to that for force,
said phos-a-phate, making it sound as though
an ejaculation. "That black green," he said,
"that's what I like to see, to see it grow."

Gardens or governments or money in the bank
or just the years, and even more than love
— lasting longer — isn't this the choicest fraud we know:
whatever we mean by growing, whatever it makes
a symbol of for us? It isn't the growth.
Just now, with nothing growing that matters at all,
I feel the most irrational happiness.

He kept a cat would eat cooked corn
and raw tomatoes. In May, he fixed the first
asparagus for it, which only shows we find
someone or something to seem to do what we can't.
The last I knew, the cat was still alive.

THE RIVER THROUGH THE MANGROVE SWAMP

Naturally, mountains and the ocean, yes, two
as terminals though not visible.
Nobody means to deny them, yet all that appears
is the dead level drawn flat and slick as plate
stretched beyond thinness to nothing: it is not there
but divides the upper from the lower world, reflects
from one to the other — which is which? These trees
have roots from their branches and their branches are under them
and sky under, blue down under, one
tangle: roots and branches, water, sky,
and somewhere suspended, unrippled clarity
which continues on, unending. Appearances.
The boat rides on the reflecting level as we
on appearances. Things are not what they seem.
No, it is true, things are not what they seem,
how much the less, are what we say they are.

4

THE SCRUTINY

That it cohere is why I look at it.
At something there. That there. As though it were.
That it were you. You is wanted. You there.
"Oh," I would say, "you there," (if you were there)
"do you know the way it is?" I want to say
how so. To tell you. If it cohered,
cohered to you, if you were there, to say,
"Oh, it is not the way we say it is,
not that. Oh, no; that way isn't the way."

OF THE SEVERAL NAMES WHICH ARE GOD'S

A man putting pole-bean seeds in the ground in May
feels a creeping sneer that thus and in other ways
the vestiges of certain orders persist.

Shouldn't we plant maybe by moonlight — or dark —
in January, hard in the icy clods?

But disorder makes its point in just this way,
by inconsistencies.

There have been dreams
having to do with landscapes, journeys there.

Their recurrence again would be the cue to refuse
to heed them, the way we pass in the street
whom once we knew, to whom we once were known.

I stand completely exposed; no defense
is any longer capable of help.

And no one attacks me. The attack is where it has gone.

AGAINST BIOGRAPHY

We came to where the trees, if there were trees,
say, a little group of them, or a house
maybe, something there, whatever it was,
a man standing, someone, it would be clear
enough, sharp at the edges, but everything else
was blurred, all running together or else
moving — sideways, back and forth — or the scale
was wrong, some of the things close by
were smaller than those set farther back, so that though
we saw something, and saw it plain enough,
we saw it nowhere, there wasn't any place
for it to be, or any place for us.
We wandered. Not quite aimless. Man here, though,
would live without biography; it needs
a time and place: there isn't any: who
could say, not smiling, me and my world
or so and so and his time, and stage a play
clothed properly in front of sets,
and believe that this made time and place of the world?

No, we had come too far for that belief
and saw ourselves as ghosts against the real,
and time and place as ghosts; there is the real.
It is there. Where we are: nowhere. It is there.

THE BODY OF THIS LIFE

I lie along the body of this life,
all night stilling my breath to listen to breath,
feeling its weight heavy against my weight.
Awake, in early light, I look at it
and set my eyes to search its hollows out,
its curves and surfaces, sojourning there
as walkers quarter whose aimless walks are a kind
of office in which they read the proper of the day,
slowing at pools of light under the trees,
impelled to certain roads, bemused at flowers,
as little knowing what a place should mean
or what they meant to find as I with you,
still sleeping, mute to me, or, waking now,
awake to some desire not my desire
and helpless to answer mine which puzzles itself
pondering what day that it were proper to
were here, that it should see in sets of bone,
in skin, in streaks of hair, some different sight
as if it were there and it not there,
nor know, at all, what sight it is it sees.

THE RECEPTORS

Were there, indeed, some *there* in the world, some *then*,
I had to be here, be there, be everywhere,
be now, and then be now and then again.

If, so to say, there were *I*, the I there were
were like those replicated houses — alike
but made to look as though unlike as with
a different color roof, a panel of brick
in front, the rooms reversed, but all alike.

Supposing person, time and place, we suppose
a redundant clumsiness, a multiple lie
that has to be told all over again, and again,
compulsive serial, to prop itself.

Great oddities: people from far away,
recluses, special vocations, rich and poor,
roles they play. But the drabbest role is role,
the oddest retreat a path we cautiously make
together to the common unrational, the sane.

I am nothing nowhere; when I move, nothing moves,
nowhere stays. It is to not pretend.
Not I nor the world. These words though.
Let there be something hard, something strict
to speak between us, thin hypotheses.

But we receive, are receptors, the world, we,
such as we are — supposed, impossible.
Anger impinges on us, beauties, fear,
received from somewhere: the words speak of these.

THE WAY

There is the world, we say, and mean a kind
of mechanism, big machine that stands
there mornings when we come on. We check the gauge
and pull a lever we learned to pull, and wait,
and stuff comes out. We put stuff in. And wait.
Nights, we go home and rest. After a while of this,
we stop; and, mornings, someone else comes on.

This is a way we made to look at things.
The way is always there, you can bank on that,
though the flow of the slot is fuller here or there
or it dwindles away. We scheme then, over moves
to make more stuff come out, or a trick technique
to overlay whole sections like a new
machine, devise a way: it works somehow.

These changes are written down: what ones were made
and who served where and when — how many days.
It makes it seem more real except that real
is what it doesn't seem at all: the skips
at night, the end a blank. What went wrong?
It isn't the way things are, but only a way
we made to look at things, among various ways.

It has rewards: the pellets of food we get
are the soothing boon of problems and problems solved
because they were solvable. We grasp at that.
We wish it might be so who sleep and die
— do what we call those names, not knowing what
we do, yet wanting a life outside the one
that sleeping drifts toward, death illuminates.

THE CORNER BY THE POST OFFICE, LATE AFTERNOON

On the far bank, a group of trees and the light
glowing from under them, from off the snow
as if it were buried there, under the snow
and signaled to us to tell us, secretly.

How inarticulate the earth is.
Always messages for us, the mouths move
and no sound or untranslatable sound.
We feel inadequate: is it our fault?

How one hill hides behind the other or one
slips out. Significant silences
like fingers that point. They call us. Demand we tell.
Good Christ! I never heard; what should I tell?

And the leaves on the lawn in summer, turning this way,
then that, breezes repointing them. Ourselves
like the leaves: something goes on: ourselves.
We watch uncomprehending. What do we say?

ON LIFE AND DEATH: SLEEP THE INTERCESSOR

I step into death; (I take it it may be death,
though step is not the word) then out again.
More, so to say, as to sleep, or exactly so:
no movement of mine, but sleep comes over me.
It seems completely right. Yes, I am he.
I smile and nod. The sought-for found. I'm here.
Is sleep the seeker? I looked, though, everywhere.
As I look now at death, the way we look
at a house we plan to move into: we stand
in the rooms only to stand in the rooms. That the rooms
should fit us, that we should fit the rooms. We think
of that to move us into the house. That door
— an inward or outward door? And the window there.
What does it look out to? What shape are the rooms?
We go; come back; are easier day by day,
for this has been our house though we lived away
in a false and smaller place to shun this house
— reverberant room after room however we go.
Its spaciousness is what we hardly dare
and what we ran from once to a little place
we made between two ends and called it place
as though it were, as though our life were there.
Death house, I come to you now for life
if there be life for us, if we may live.

THE REAL SURROUNDING: ON CANALETTO'S VENICE

Turner ended dazzled: all he saw
was the concentration of light. There is something to say
besides glory all the time. Gloria!
And Canaletto saw what else there is.
There is, with him, a certain meticulousness
— windows are counted, cornices scrupulous,
even reflections rectilinear.
He set it down "the way it is" as the phrase
asserts it is which, in a sense, is true.
In a world of illusionists, he was prepared
to repeat the terms of illusion just as they were,
to treat the straitest phantasies as if
he thought they were true, as he might have wanted them true
and there they are: facade and tower, dome
and weathervane just as they said they were,
this house and then this house and this one next,
all carefully rendered, recognizable,
in back of what he meant we should see. He said,
"Look at the emptiness. All this air."
He said, "It confronts us; this is what there is."
He felt an urgency to paint it there
as a positive presence, not as something gone.
The real surrounding is a medium more than man
can will, despoil, or even reckon with.
It sets us free. The world is not our world,
and what we make for a world is simply that
not more, not less. Let be. And the emptiness!
The space around us. We are lost in it. Its winds
infuse our willessness. It seems we are there
by not being there. In the picture again, see how
his boats and boatmen dissolve in the luminous air.

THE CONTINUANCE

The time they misdirected themselves to a wake
and, coming to the coffin, found a corpse of the wrong sex
who was no one they knew, they knelt and nuzzled their fists.

It was get out, of course, without guffaw
and around the corner to where they should have been
but helpless with hidden laughter the whole time.
They cherished the joke; in the back of their minds, even more,
was the look of the roomfull of faces they didn't know.
The separate cruelty.

How almost all
of life is unspeakable. Disjunctiveness.
They thought of that. Incongruence.

It seems
as though, on a journey, we wake in the night. We must
have stopped somewhere — no telling where. In the light,
we look at the others, look at ourselves, invent
procedures to pass time, are as intent
at this as if we came for the purpose. The rules
change. It is uncertain what they are. We go on.

ON THE FAILURE OF MEANING IN THE ABSENCE OF OBJECTIVE ANALOGS

There was a message in a place where messages are.
One of the places. It might have been anywhere else
except for the message there. I make the rounds.
Nothing usually. Like running a line
as is said of trappers running a line for skins.
Not much there but just the same we do.
The message: it said I wasn't going to miss
much, being gone; there wasn't any big
event to happen. I thought it must be true.
I hadn't any way to know; but this was true.
It meant it didn't matter when to die:
that time was all, that this was all of time
whether we thought it came to a stop with us
or thought there was nothing of us or it to stop,
the same would stay the same if staying was
for, more than likely, 'staying' was wrong to say.
If something stayed then something else must move
and nothing moves — like going — nothing moves.
The thing to stay for wasn't going to be.
So look around and what there is is here.

The message: I read it over again.
The messages we get we write ourselves
but even so. It doesn't so much mean
there isn't a big event as it means that big
event or little, the idea of coming is wrong.
There is only this whatever this may mean
and this is what there is and nothing will be.

Or again not. A message is meaningless
in the end: not wrong but meaningless.
As language is. The clarity that words
can make is not about the world — where it looks
to see itself and is lost, not seeing there.
It sees disparity: despairs of words.

THE PLAINEST NARRATIVE

I am William Bronk, have been raised to believe
the personal pronoun plus the verb to be
and a proper name said honestly is fact
from which the plainest narrative begins.
But it isn't fact; it comes to this. Is it wrong?
Not wrong. Just that it isn't true.
No more than the opposite is true. That "I" —
as arbitrary as the proper name, a role
assumed from the verb to be as though to be
were all assumption, were willed; and of course it is
and anyone fooled is fooled. Do as you will.
It doesn't matter. What happens to us is not
what happens. It isn't by us. We feel it there.
Listen. Something is living. It is not we.
Aren't we that Adam, still, from whom we are?
The garden is here. I have no way to eat,
have never eaten. I round that fruit.
I push against the branches of that tree.

16

THE MEDIUM MOVES

It is hard to wish now for a long life.
One lost belief is in length as such.
What do we want of it? Isn't what we make
a secretion of process merely: an oyster shell,
the life the same oyster, always the same?
That pale softness. What would more mean?
Pearls are not the point. Somebody's pearl world!
Perdurable. No. The blob of it.
That grey dab as if for nothing, as if
for always. Though, so to say, the water moves
a little. Water colors. Seems to move.
Sleeping or waking, not much of life is life.

THE MEETING GROUND

Sleep is limper, has a suppler skin
than waking, lies that much nearer in against
whatever there is that, in death, ingests
us, as something does, whatever it is that does.
We are wakers but wakers who sleep, sleepers who die,
and of those states there isn't much we know
but that they meet each other and we are the ground
somehow on which they meet: the meeting ground.
Not something on that ground — we *are* the ground.
Or again, as though *they were* and we
lay over them, too close to separate,
are what they are, all three, and they are we.

Except as sleep informs it, waking is what
we sometimes mean by death, a place apart,
a going away. Come closer in: we are
the death we die, we live awake with it
and sleeping, search it out. I wake in the night.
Mornings the same. Sleep opens me.
My watchfulness. Naked. As in a door.

GRAFFITI ON THE GROUND IN THE NASCA DESERT

"They extend for miles." So it is said of them.
Another one says, "In the end, they fade into nothing."
Men are depicted, various beasts; but lines
are the typical work, as though measured increase in one
direction were something (well, something) if nothing more.

One thinks of rods and chains, of ladders, dynasties,
high buildings, throughway mileposts, all the things
accrued and finial in the face of emptiness,
extension, as in this empty extension here.

Is there nothing else we can say? — even to eyes
assumed as far away as they assumed eyes
to see a message too close for them to see?

WHERE WE ARE; OR GETTING THERE IS ONLY HALF THE FUN

Travel comes to an end. We get to there
wherever it claims to be, or home again,
and it's over. That's all of that. Travel assumes
that place is different from place, though everyone knows
(even the traveler knows) the assumption is made
mostly to make the trip, to offer excuse
for it, for what we want: the travel, the steps
from here to there, the demands, their peremptoriness,
preemption. Dear God! That something engage us, that we
be busy at something, wars or careers, enroute!
Going somewhere. Moving again so as not
to have time for here, not to be stuck with it.
With here. Look at it! At here. Let's go!

20

WHAT ABOUT US?

We look for clues and nothing is trivial
unless the publicly labeled certainties
we know to be false.

                But falseness, itself, is a help.
At least, sometimes: how desire, we know, deceives
us, detailing its lust in the wildest improbables
which we lead ourselves to believe will really be there.
And when we fail, — we do, we always fail,
we find the wildest improbables were real
and what we wanted. Though not here. And we still do.
It's a place to start. It's something. It isn't much.
But what do we know? It tells us something to say.

ALICE SAID SHE WAS CLIMBING THE WALLS. WELL I KNOW WHAT SHE MEANS

Why don't you say something to me which both of us know is nothing and I know that you know. Say, "There, now." That should do it.
                    You haven't got it to say.
I haven't either.
                    Why don't you say, "There, there."

LEAVING YOU

Be what you will; I mean to be less than I was.
Or less, at least, than what I thought to be.
It wasn't likely; yours was another mind
never complaisant with me, nor seeing what I
saw. The end we reach isn't the end of much.

Say I go back to being my own man,
the man I go back to is much less man.
I declare the loss. Let the credit from it accrue
to the common fund. As it will. I acquiesce.
What will you do? What shall you make of yours?

OF THE NATURAL WORLD

Of the natural world, nothing is possible
but praise if we speak at all. We can be still.

The steadiest speakers are quiet after a time.

I could be quiet now and not wait for the time
when the quiet comes except that so little sound
is hardly to be heard in the loud joy of the world
and I grow impatient and practice the world's song.

AT FIFTY

Grotesque at fifty to be probationer
of love, reporting at designated times
to any officer as may be designate
or casually, seeing the chance appear.

Progressively more ghostly, in ghostly arms
grasping some ghostliness. Empty despair.

That ghost should feel the iron of soft viscera
and beat what might have been its fists on the wall!

That desire holds! That, at fifty, what I said
at twenty should still be true! That in thirty years
no one should show me wrong! I was wrong! I was wrong!

CONJECTURAL READING

I read it wrong. It wouldn't help to say
I didn't invent the reading, that all I did
was read it the way that anyone else would read,
the way that tradition established, the only way
so far as anyone knew. I read it so wrong
that — Is there tradition? — the idea seems dubious.
Who is the everyone else that reads, and who,
indeed, is the I to be wrong? It might be said
— Lew used to say it — I wasn't even wrong.

Oh, it was "rational" as the term says,
meaning: I am; the world is;
there are other people; and they are; we begin
and end; there is a middle somewhere between;
in the middle something happens and this is the point;
we are measured by that and add our measure to all.

The trouble with rational is, it seems to make sense,
in the end it doesn't make any sense at all.

Conjectural reading and reason reading from that.
We read the language wrong. These words are not
the words; syntax misses. May I hear it again?
There has to be some way to read so it says:
it is unmeasurable; the whole is here;
there is nothing to come; it neither was nor will be.

THE GREED

In bed. Asleep. Or half asleep: awake
in sleep to a consciousness we grope against
in waking.
           It's all right. Morning will come,
crows crying in the yard and the branches of trees
shaking, waving some.
           We look at the light,
rise, let light and water wash across
our darkness. Pleasure. The little things. Sport
of the world. But even so.
           Afterwards,
take me to bed with you. Let me sleep.
I am greedy after sleep's consciousness.

THAT SOMETHING THERE IS SHOULD BE

Things have; we have no history:
we are men. You are a woman, but even so.
No, even so. It sounds like a kind of joke,
but that's what I mean: we are human. Human is not
to be something we know, but to be as the Jews say God
must be, without an image. What happens takes
no care for how we look, what part we take,
or whether we can. Something there is will be.
Caress me, be kind. We have no history.

SOMETHING LIKE TEPEES

Glances and recollections, letters of sorts
is what we get from each other. Rose called.

I had forgotten. Well, no I hadn't. I'd stopped
expecting. We learn. Not much. Not finally.

We learn. That we aren't, as we thought we were, alone.
There are others here. All right. It isn't much.

Remember once. There was a time we meant
to make something like tepees, I out of you,

you from me, and live there, make it home
as though to make a house were what we meant.

Journeys do not end in lovers meeting.
Nor end. Sometimes we touch and touch again.

MAKING IT

Shirley thinks it is somehow our fault:
a gap in the guts, our luck, some guilty slip
we made, or we that are made wrong. We missed.
God help us; it could be so. I say it's not.
And nobody else's fault, or even a fault.
It's the way it is. People make it. They do.
It's possible. But here is what they make:
is there only this? It isn't the point. The point
is not to. The point is to know that.

THE ABNEGATION

I want to be that Tantalus, unfed
forever, that my want's agony declare
that such as we want has nothing to say to the world;
if the world wants, it nothing wants for us.
Let me be unsatisfied. Hearing me scream,
spare me compassion, look instead at man,
how he takes handouts, makeshifts, sops
for creature comfort. I refuse. I will not
be less than I am to be more human, or less
than human may be to seem to be more than I am.
I want as the world wants. I am the world.

YES: I MEAN SO OK — LOVE

Some people say, "Well good,
now you write about love."

"Yes," I say, "what else,
I always have; what else?"

"You don't understand," they say,
"I mean love; that's what it's about."

"Yes," I say, "about love,
but that's not what I mean."

WRITING YOU

What I should do is phone; the circuitry
is there and we're both somewhere in the circuitry.
I need to talk. What should I find to say?
You know how it is: it rings; you answer; no click;
no dial tone. Hello? Hello? No word.
Not even goodbye — I couldn't give you that.

Listen to this: to write you requires a scheme,
subtends an apparatus, such that here
be an I, you be he there, space
discerns the entities, depicts them such
as the scheme requires. Are you lost? I am.
I want to be not lost. I write even so.

Tell me what to do. I want to show.
Schemelessness. Undress. To speak from that.
I want the secrecy; I want it said.
To speak from wordlessness. There are certain things
that happen and we don't know: proteins meet
and shape each other. We are the husk of this.

Whatever happens happens in some such wise,
under attention. I hate all huskiness.
Let me be where it happens, let me be the hidden cells
and silent if silence is all there is to say.
I want to talk though. I want to talk to you.
I despair of what to say. Goodnight. Goodnight.

I THOUGHT IT WAS HARRY

Excuse me. I thought for a moment you were someone I know.
It happens to me. One time at *The Circle in the Square*
when it *was* still in the Square, I turned my head
when the lights went up and saw me there with a girl
and another couple. Out in the lobby, I looked
right at him and he looked away. I was no one he knew.
Well, it takes two, as they say, and I don't know what
it would prove anyway. Do we know who we are,
do you think? Kids seem to know. One time I asked
a little girl. She said she'd been sick. She said
she'd looked different and felt different. I said,
"Maybe it wasn't you. How do you know?"
"Oh, I was me," she said, "I know I was."

That part doesn't bother me anymore
or not the way it did. I'm nobody else
and nobody anyway. It's all the rest
I don't know. I don't know anything.
It hit me. I thought it was Harry when I saw you
and thought, "I'll ask Harry." I don't suppose
he knows, though. It's not that I get confused.
I don't mean that. If someone appeared and said,
"Ask me questions," I wouldn't know where to start.
I don't have questions even. It's the way I fade
as though I were someone's snapshot left in the light.
And the background fades the way it might if we woke
in the wrong twilight and things got dim and grey
while we waited for them to sharpen. Less and less
is real. No fixed point. Questions fix
a point, as answers do. Things move again
and the only place to move is away. It was wrong:
questions and answers are what to be without
and all we learn is how sound our ignorance is.
That's what I wanted to talk to Harry about.
You looked like him. Thank you anyway.

THE TORMENT

I am that bull they bait, this way, that way,
head down, stupid, off to the side of the ring.
Who are they? They fade to the fence whenever I charge.
Let them watch out! I think I am in disguise.
There may be nothing more if I am gone.

THE BEING

The bush did burn. The tablets, in the end,
were blank for Moses' guesses. But it did burn.

They were with the tree. I denied them the fruit of the tree
but they were there with it. Mine was the image they showed.

Son? There are many sons. He had a name.
I am the nameless one. I am who am.

Not one of those. Not given. Not anywhere.

THE INCARNATION

I come back to my body as if to my own place
who am elsewhere landless. I go the long way
whose going is more a staying. They come to me
the places not place, the nowhere places;
I have no belief to give them. They are there. No doubt
they are there. Incredulous, undone, I toss
from one to another one and remember back
to places I might have made: O, the sweet
valleys, homely worlds. Gone and well gone.
Body help me! Tell me where I am.

VENI CREATOR SPIRITUS

If one were all, there were still the want to be
something. The wanting something. One says all
or nothing; something is in between but not
halfway. All and nothing meet, conjoin,
speak of the same, as circumference and area
speak of the same circle. Something across
from there, something besides, as if besides
one, there were numbers besides. One wishes there were.

THE OPPOSITION

All right! So it doesn't make any sense; we still
are disposed to talk about it in terms as best
we may, and that means rational. If not
to make sense, what are we talking for? And yet
we have to know that what we talk about
is more, is less — is other — than rational.

All the opposition there is in the world
is nothing much to this one: the way we try
to talk in sensible terms — what else? — of what
we know escapes (and we want it to) from sense.
Suppose, for example, we were born, as we say we are,
and died, in the end, after a reasonable life:

No would be all I could say to that, which I want
more than anything else that I could want.

THE STORY OF MANKIND FROM EARLIEST TIMES TO THE PRESENT DAY

We are so set on making stories, asleep
even, only the mind moving, lying intent
to stroke whatever comes to it, awake
while the body sleeps, identifying sounds
with events, feelings with faces, picking out
from the day's debris whatever will make do.

Awake, our invention finds more room to move,
sets up itself in three dimensions as if
it were there, assigns us almost consistent roles
to hold from day to day, necessitates
a past we must have had, and a time to come
where, even now, the story begins to be true.

What may, in fact, go on, if indeed it does,
has nothing at all to take from the story we tell.

CIVITAS DEI

When it was plain that there was never to be
the City of God; after the line was clear
that there was no line and none ever to be made;
when it was plain that nothing at all was plain,
we looked from side to side, we turned back,
and no way there either, and here we were.

Yes, and here we are. Nowhere to go.
Already here because such as cities are
is such as the city of god can ever be
or, if there is meaning, such as was meant to be.
Hocus pocus, here is what there is:
one side of the street looks at the other side.

Among the magniloquent monuments of once joys
we walk with our long familiars: dread, disdain.

THE MASK THE WEARER OF THE MASK WEARS

Yes, look at me; I am the mask it wears,
as much am that which is within the mask.
Nothing not mask but that. That every mask.

The mask will fall away and nothing lost.
There is only the mask-wearer, the self-aware,
the only aware, aware of only the self.

Awake, it dreams: is every character;
is always more; is never only that.
It contemplates; tries any mask of shape.

Any is nothing. Any is not what is.
But that it should be. That it should seem to be.
That it be no more than that, and yet should be.

And that it turn to look, look favorably,
look lovingly, look long, on what there is.

IN PRAISE OF LOVE

Unless to you, to whom should I praise love?
It is a throwaway, a breath on the air,
gratuitous, as if not elicited.

And how should I feel the absence, the emptiness,
the failure to be there except as someone not?
It was you, that one, the one not there.

MYSTERY TRANSCENDENT

Your suggestion of four o'clock Tuesday: be sure I'll be there
on the hour, and the Tuesday anyone else's as well.
As you may know, and I say it to savor that,
I stopped with watches some time ago. Retreats,
as they say, little concessions, on both sides,
the positions no less directly opposite
but not pushed now to ends that, — well,
how could they end? I was the one, of course,
who made the concessions. Do you know why?
I gather you may. That it isn't only time,
that all the issues clearly drawn are, dread
shall we say? Are horror? Are terrible? You know
about the horror, don't you? And the mystery:
transcendence, position abandoned. Tuesday. Four.

I AM

Joy
which is neither
because
nor in spite of
but is
joy

and despair
which neither
was
nor will be
but is
all.

THE AGGRANDIZEMENT: it's a short road that has no turnoff

On the street.
Hey.
Come here.
You.
I want you.

Or
enviable.

As though the hands
(my hands)
should love the face
(my face).

Not it's *mine*.
It's *me*.
That's that.

Sweet Jesus!
To know that!

THE USE-UNUSE OF US

At Charlie Carleton's farm, which several more
have claimed since it was his, and Charlie dead
for years. He must have been.

                              Look at it there;
the group the buildings make. Only the house
used now and that not much.
The barns idle. Their sides. Sag a little.
But there it is. The group. Only its shape.
As if its shape were all it meant to be.
Nothing ever besides.

                              Did Charlie build
the place? He put it to use. Use it must
have meant to him. And of course, *it* using him.

What uses who? Who what? As if
something were said, we don't catch what.

We are used or not used; and, Charlie, I think
it doesn't matter. Anyway, nobody asks
us, Charlie. No use to. We ask ourselves.

THE UNBELIEVABLE

We are made afraid not to believe the fraud
of this world: believe or be lost.

                              Lost anyway.
No more to lose. Not that we ever had.
We said we had. The world said. It said,
"There is a world for having, a world to be had:
only believe." Who was had?

                            World,
I say no. No world.

                      These are not
spoken speeches. Nobody says, or to say.

But the unbelievable, which nothing believes,
says something. Listen. Says itself.
As if it were my voice. As if it were now.

JUNE COMES, JANUS FACED

The house this morning stands to the south of the sun.
I am there and see it: sun on the north side.

The new illumine plays us the scene reversed.
We face and look backwards, are solider.

Evenings, I walk the canal, skinning its feel.
The water's warm courses lavish me.

How shall we bear the green? It is possible.
The lawn, the placed leaves. They stifle us.

THE WONDER OF OUR CONTRARIETY

How moving they are, the houses with the awninged, wide
porches, children in them, lights at night.

Macbeth's wonder: "Can such things be?" he asked,
seeing ghosts. The lack of wonder puzzled him.

Houses are ghostly strange. How do we dare?
A bold story, the fiction of our lives

which assumes "there once was a man who . . ." as though
it were only the plainest form of matter of fact,

whereas what is plain is the invention of it, the lie
if you like, the contrariety. We know.

What we know is our failure to compose: that our being is
and is unalterable. No changing that.

We build these houses, these temporalities,
gone in a little as their children are gone. Gone.